Sweet Smelling Stories

igloobooks

This igloo book belongs to:

....

My Sweetest Fairy Story

igloobooks

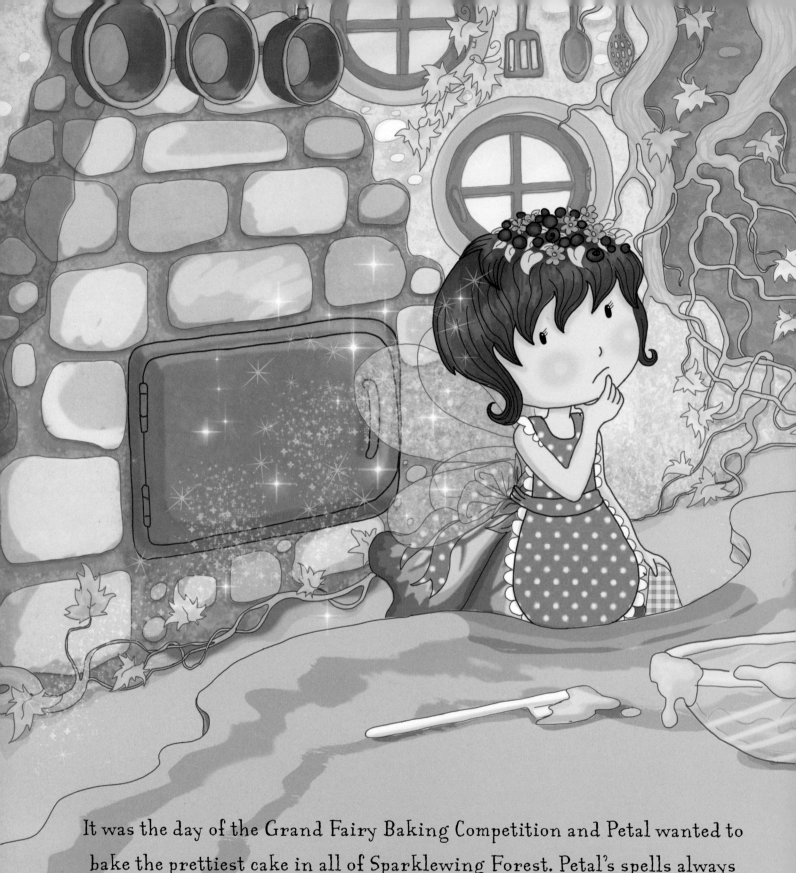

It was the day of the Grand Fairy Baking Competition and Petal wanted to bake the prettiest cake in all of Sparklewing Forest. Petal's spells always seemed to go wrong, so instead of using magic, she decided to make a cake all by herself. First, she baked layers of vanilla sponge.

Once the cake was baked, Petal mixed a big bowl of pink, vanilla icing and poured it on top with a SPLODGE. "Hmm," thought Petal. "Vanilla just isn't very exciting. Maybe I should find something to add to it." Then, she had a wonderful idea. "I'll use some strawberries from the forest."

Fairy Petal flew as fast as her wings would carry her to the strawberry patch. "No one else knows about the lovely, juicy strawberries that grow at the edge of the forest," she thought to herself. When Petal arrived at the patch, she gasped with surprise.

The strawberries were nearly all gone! Fairy Rosa was fluttering nearby, with two baskets piled high with yummy strawberries. "Sorry for taking all these, Petal," said Rosa, shyly. "I need them to make my special strawberry tart for the baking competition. I hope you don't mind."

Petal decided to collect lemons from the trees on Daisy Hill instead,
but by the time she got there, Pixie Luna and her brothers and sisters
had already picked them all. "We're making fizzy lemon cupcakes
for the baking competition," said Luna. "Sorry, Petal."

"Grandma has an orange tree outside her cottage," thought Petal.
"I could use those instead!" Petal fluttered to Grandma's cottage, but Grandma
had already given the oranges to her neighbour, Fairy Clementine.
"Clementine is entering the competition, too," said Grandma.
"She's making an orange drizzle cake!"

Petal fluttered home sadly, with an empty basket. How would she make her vanilla cake more exciting now? "Maybe I could use a little bit of magic to make it more special," she thought. Petal got her wand and, concentrating hard, cast a spell to make some sparkly icing.

SPLOOSH! Icing came flying out of Petal's wand. She tried
her hardest to control the sparkly swirls, but they splattered over the
table and the cake in big squiggles. "Oh, no!" cried Petal. Her cake
looked even worse now than it had done before.

The iced cake looked like so much of a mess that Petal wanted to cry.
She tried desperately to think of something else that her cake could be
decorated with. It had to be something wonderful and sparkly,
so that the judges wouldn't notice the messy icing.

"I know! I could use glittery fairy dust," said Petal. She grabbed a jar and tipped it over her cake. To Petal's surprise, the sparkles started to whizz and whoosh through the sponge. Petal realised that she had grabbed a jar of mini shooting stars by mistake!

Now, Petal's cake was covered in big holes, where the shooting
stars had whizzed their way through it. "I've got to try something else,"
said Petal, swishing her wand all over the place in a panic.
"Maybe I could make some beautiful sugar butterflies."

Petal cast a magic spell, thinking that butterflies would
cover up the missing chunks and the messy icing. Suddenly, hundreds of
butterflies appeared, but instead of settling on the cake, they fluttered up
into the air and right out of Petal's open window.

"Come back!" cried Petal, chasing the butterflies outside. "Oh, I should never have used magic on my cake!" Petal was so upset that she didn't look where she was going. She flew straight into a tree trunk with a THUMP. Then, something fell from the tree, right onto Petal's head.

Petal looked down at the grass and saw a shiny, red cherry.
Then, she looked up and gasped. The whole tree was covered in the most
delicious-looking cherries. "Perfect to a make a whole new cake with,"
giggled Petal. She gathered up lots of cherries and flew back to her kitchen.

Petal didn't have long to make her cherry cake. The baking competition would be starting in no time at all. She threw her old cake into the garden for the birds to eat, then whipped, whizzed and whisked up some new ingredients until she had a brand new batch of cake mixture.

Petal chopped up the juicy
cherries and whirled them
into some sugary icing.
"I hope this works,"
said Petal, feeling very
nervous as the first layer
of sponge baked, but there
was no need to worry.
The cherry cake smelled so
delicious that animals
from all around came
to see what it was.

When Petal's cherry cake was baked, she built it up into a
tower, with fruity, cherry cream between the sponge and
lots of sticky, cherry icing on top. Then, she placed
cherries all around the edge. The cake looked
wonderful and Petal felt very proud.

In fact, Petal was feeling so confident that she decided
to try one last magic spell. She swished her sparkly, star-shaped
wand over one of the cherries. SWOOSH! Suddenly, the cherry
was enormous. "Perfect," giggled Petal, carefully placing
the giant cherry on top of her cake.

Petal checked the time and gasped. The Grand Fairy Baking Competition was about to begin. She grabbed her cherry cake and fluttered as fast as she could across the flower fields. The cake wibbled and wobbled as Petal flew into the marquee with all of the other contestants.

Everyone placed their cakes next to one another along
the judging table. Petal looked at everyone else's cakes and felt worried.
"My cake doesn't look very nice compared to Clementine's orange drizzle
cake and Rosa's strawberry tart," she thought, sadly. "The pixies'
cupcakes look so sparkly and yummy, too."

The fairy judges tasted the different cakes. When they reached Petal,
she handed them each a big, gooey slice of sticky cherry cake.
Petal made sure that every judge got a whole cherry on their plate, too.
As they each tasted Petal's cake, the judges stopped
and looked at one another in surprise.

"This cake is delicious!" cried one of the judges.
"What spell did you use to bake it, Petal?"
"Yes, you must tell us which charms you used," said another, excitedly.
Petal giggled. "Well, I only used one spell to make a giant cherry. All of my
other spells kept going wrong, so I baked the cake from scratch instead."

Soon, the judges were ready to announce the winner of the Grand
Fairy Baking Competition. "Our winner today is the fairy who worked
the hardest out of everyone," said the head judge. "Petal, your cherry
cake, made without magic, has won first prize!" Petal couldn't believe
her eyes as she was handed a lovely cupcake trophy.

"Well done, Petal!" cried everyone, with a big cheer.
All the fairies were so happy that Petal had won first prize,
even though she didn't get to use any strawberries, oranges
or lemons. Her cherry cake was so delicious that the fairies all
agreed baking really was better without any magic at all.

Can You Spot?

Can you work out which pages these items appear on?
They are hidden throughout this super-sweet story.

Can you find this heart-topped cake?

Did you spot this lemon-collecting pixie?

Where did you see this starry sign?

Do you remember these dotty birds?

Did you spot this yummy chocolate?

Can you spot this surprised mouse?

Do you remember this magical jar?

Did you spot this magical-wand box?

The End!

My Sweetest
Princess
Story

Princess Polly loved to eat strawberries more than anything else
in the world. For breakfast, she would gobble down stacks of strawberry
pancakes, with oozy strawberry sauce. Then, she would munch a
couple of sticky, pink strawberry cupcakes.

The king and queen were worried about Polly. "Don't you want to try eating other things, without strawberries?" they asked the princess, as she slurped down a thick, gloopy strawberry milkshake. "No, thank you," said Princess Polly. "Strawberries are the best."

After breakfast, Princess Polly usually wanted to eat even more strawberry treats. She would sneak to the kitchen, where the royal chef would happily make her a strawberry sundae, or strawberry sandwiches. He sometimes even made strawberry pizza, with extra-sugary sauce.

Princess Polly munched her way through so many strawberries that she even had her own strawberry fields, stretching right across the palace grounds. "I'm so happy to have so many strawberries all to myself," thought Princess Polly, gazing out of her bedroom window.

Then, one day, something terrible happened. Princess Polly was out walking with the king and queen, when she spotted a gigantic flock of birds circling above her strawberry fields. "I wonder what they're doing," Polly thought to herself, looking up at the sky curiously.

Suddenly, hundreds of birds swooped down and started to snatch up
Princess Polly's strawberries with their beaks. "Stop it!" shrieked Polly.
"Leave my strawberries alone!" The greedy birds didn't listen. In no time
at all, they had gobbled down every last one of Polly's strawberries.

Without strawberries, Princess Polly refused to eat anything at all.
The king and queen tried to think of ways to tempt Polly into eating
something new. "Don't worry," said the royal chef. "I'll cook some
fantastic new dishes." Soon, he had filled the dining table
with strange and exciting meals.

"Try this pizza covered with sweets, Polly," suggested the queen. "Or some chicken, with a squashy pink marshmallow," said the king. The chef brought the princess crunchy carrot cupcakes and a cherry and chocolate swiss roll. He even made jelly with chips and a raspberry and sausage tart, but Polly just crossed her arms and frowned.

Later, after lots of banging about in the kitchen, the royal chef wheeled out an enormous cake. It was covered in purple jelly and stuffed full of peanuts. "I made my very special peanut butter and jelly cake just for you, Princess," said the royal chef, puffing out his chest proudly.

Princess Polly thought the cake looked horrible. It didn't have any strawberries in it at all. She gave it a little poke and with a big SQUISH, a blob of purple jelly came squelching from the cake and splatted right onto Princess Polly's face.

Princess Polly took the cake from the royal chef, but only so that everyone would leave her alone. "I'm not eating that mountain of peanut gloop, Smudge," she told her puppy. "It hasn't got any strawberries in it at all." To Smudge's delight, Princess Polly gave him slice after slice of peanut cake, until the whole thing had gone.

That evening, the king and queen were holding a grand feast and
everyone was busy preparing for the guests to arrive. The royal seamstress
had even made Princess Polly a special dress to wear. When the queen
brought it up to her bedroom, Polly just cried, "There won't be any
strawberries at the feast, so I'm not going!"

As Princess Polly sat and sulked in her bedroom, she could smell all the food from the grand feast. "It's making my tummy growl and gurgle," moaned Polly. Soon, she was so hungry that she couldn't bear it, so Polly decided to creep downstairs and see if there was anything for her to eat.

When she reached the bottom of the grand staricase, Princess
Polly peeked into the dining room. She listened to all of the king and
queen's guests laughing and saying how delicious the food tasted.
As she hid behind the wall, the yummy smells became so strong
that Polly's mouth started to water.

Polly wanted to get a better look at the dishes that the guests were eating. "Why does everything smell so tasty, when there isn't a single strawberry in sight?" she wondered. Quietly, the princess crept into the dining room. Before anybody noticed, she crawled underneath the table to hide.

Princess Polly peeked over the dining table and couldn't believe
how many unusual things she could see. Everything looked amazing!
Sneakily, Polly snatched a bowl of blueberries, some chocolate cupcakes,
a few sandwiches and a hot dog, then scrambled back under the table.

First, Princess Polly decided to try a gooey chocolate cupcake. She took a
small bite and couldn't believe how scrummy the chocolate icing was!
After gobbling down the rest of the cupcake, Polly nibbled her way
through a crunchy cucumber sandwich, which was very tasty, too.

Next, Polly ate an extra-saucy hot dog, dripping with mustard and tomato sauce. Smudge was enjoying the food from the feast, too. He had just munched his way through a juicy peach, when Princess Polly grabbed a handful of plump blueberries from the bowl. Wondering what exactly they were, she popped a berry into her mouth. "Wow!" cried Polly. "This is even yummier than a strawberry!"

Princess Polly suddenly realised that she had spoken very loudly. Everyone must have heard her! "Who's under the table?" said one of the guests, sounding puzzled. The king lifted up the long tablecloth and saw Polly underneath, with blueberry juice all around her mouth.

"What on earth are you hiding under the table for, Polly?" asked
the queen. Feeling embarrased, Princess Polly told the queen how hungry
she had been and how much she liked the blueberries. "They're delicious,"
she said. "I'm sorry for not trying to eat the food you brought me earlier."

The next day, Princess Polly couldn't wait until dinner time. The royal chef whipped up every lovely dish that Polly had refused before, plus lots of extra-special treats. There was a blueberry tart, a blueberry pie and even a blueberry sundae. "Oh, thank you!" said Polly to the royal chef.

"I'm glad that the birds ate my strawberries," Princess Polly told the king and queen, through a mouthful of chocolate cupcake. "Otherwise, I would never have tried blueberries or peaches, or any of the other yummy things I've eaten since yesterday."

With help from the royal gardeners, Princess Polly planted all sorts of different fruit across the palace grounds. She grew juicy grapes, sweet raspberries and even the biggest watermelons in the whole kingdom.

Best of all, Princess Polly loved to share her fruit with everyone. The king and queen were very proud of Polly for trying lots of different food, but they were even prouder of what a generous princess she had become after all.

Can You Spot?

Can you work out which pages these items appear on?
They are hidden throughout this super-sweet story.

Do you remember where this tart was?

Did you notice the dolly on the floor?

Did you spot this sprinkly fountain?

Did you spot these shoes?

Did you spot this plate of watermelon?

Can you find this picture of Smudge?

Do you remember this magical lamp?

Can you find the strawberry throne?

The End!

Published in 2014
by Igloo Books Ltd
Cottage Farm
Sywell
NN6 0BJ
www.igloobooks.com

GUA006 1213
2 4 6 8 10 9 7 5 3
ISBN: 978-1-78197-328-8

Illustrated by Emma Foster

Printed and manufactured in China